For Jason M.

Tuesday, June 8th, 2021—personal journal of Jane Tokugawa

Arrived at Keflavík around 1am, direct from Atlanta. Skies overcast, reminded me of late fall in Detroit. Felipe, Jacob, and I picked up our bags, breezed through customs, took the shuttle to our hotel in Reykjavík. Randall took a private car, citing security concerns, though Iceland has remained free of the terrorism that continues to plague mainland Europe.

Plague. You would think a Center for Disease Control employee wouldn't use that word figuratively. But it's such a good word.

Our delegation has four members. Three from the CDC: myself (leading the delegation as Senior Scientist), Jacob Weisman (Ethics Program Specialist), and Felipe Hernandez (Technical Mission Support). Randall Lewis is from the State Department, Arms Control and International Security Affairs. Met him in person for the first time today, not sure what his exact title is. Gruff, bald, hard-to-read.

We're here to look into a new gene therapy treatment recently approved in Iceland, and attracting a great deal of medical tourism from the

U.S., Europe, and Asia (limited to those that can obtain a visa—Icelandic immigration control has tightened noticeably this year).

Jacob fell asleep—or pretended to—on the shuttle, and either accidentally or sneakily rested his hand against my thigh. I scooted away, making the shuttle ride even more uncomfortable (the heat was on too high—I felt nauseous). He's been passive-aggressively flirting with me since we were assigned to this team. Nothing obvious enough to confront. I want nothing to do with Jacob in that way, but I'm hoping I don't have to be blunt about it.

Felipe, on the other hand, what a cutie. Too young for anything serious, but if he finds his way to my hotel room one of these nights, I won't turn him away. We're here for nine days, investigating Ásdís Lúthersdóttir's retroviral gene therapy protocol, so there might be opportunities. Not sure if he's into nerdy half-Japanese women twice his age, but he's friendly enough. Even odds for a hookup between me and the tech.

Pressed up against the window, I lost myself in the landscape (a dozen shades of blue-green lichen clinging to dark gray rocks, no trees) and endured the ride, thinking about our mission. Ostensibly, it's to verify that

Lúthersdóttir's individually engineered retroviruses aren't contagious. But two things make me think this is a fishing expedition:

1—the presence of Randall Lewis from the State Department.

2—Lúthersdóttir started human trials back in '18, and there hasn't been even a whiff of any contagion threat. So why investigate now?

My guess? Iceland is *shining*, a brilliant, blinding star of a nation. Eighteen medals (including three gold) at the Tokyo Olympics, a stunning number for a nation of only four-hundred-thousand citizens. Three of the world's top-ten ranked chess masters. Dozens of newly world-famous musicians, actors, and authors. A thriving economy, dominating a number of niche industries (including bioengineering—thanks in no small part to patents originating from *Hratthníf*—Lúthersdóttir's lab).

It's not the CDC's job to find out what they're putting in the water in Iceland (and if Lúthersdóttir has anything to do with it) but I'm concerned that's what we'll be used to find out.

Glad I brought this journal, despite Icelandic Air's draconian weight limits. I need to get it all down, exorcise my hypergraphic compulsions.

Wednesday, June 9th, 2021

Valdimar, a serious but polite young bioengineer, gave us a tour of the Hratthníf labs (*Hratthníf* translates literally as *fast knife*—a reference to the precision-cleaving Cas9 CRISPR enzyme). The facility was unlike any lab I'd ever seen—informal, borderline unprofessional. The floor plan was completely open—no private offices or dividers of any kind, with as much room dedicated to foosball and Ping-Pong tables as workstations. Music was piped in from somewhere, at a reasonable volume but distractingly varied (I heard classical, Scandinavian death metal, American pop music, Irish folk songs). Most disconcerting was the complete lack of lab coats, containment suits, or any kind of clean protocol.

"This space is for research and modeling?" I asked. "The sequencing facility is somewhere else?"

"No," answered Valdimar, smiling. "All the viral synthesis takes place right here. *This*"—he touched a white cube-shaped appliance on a nearby desk—"is one of our proprietary assemblers."

"But the room isn't sterile."

"It doesn't need to be. The machine interior is sterile. We just add new gacked cartridges when they run low."

"Gacked?" asked Felipe.

"Sorry. G.A.C.T. amino acid cartridges. Printer ink, basically."

"When will Lúthersdóttir be joining us?" asked Randall, sounding irritated.

"She's reviewing some trial results, Mr. Lewis," said Valdimar, stiffly. "She is hoping to join us shortly. But if not, you will definitely see her tomorrow. She is greatly looking forward to introducing you to Svere Jónsson, our patient zero, if you will." With this he winked at me, disconcertingly.

"Poor choice of words," said Randall, missing the dry joke. "And that's unfortunate. We were told Lúthersdóttir would be available…"

"We look forward to meeting her," I interrupted. "And we appreciate you opening up your facility to us." Neither the nation of Iceland nor the privately owned Hratthníf corporation were legally obligated to show our delegation anything.

"Good diplomatic relations with the United States are worth a great deal to us," said Valdimar, locking eyes with me. Thirty seconds ago I would have identified his tone as sincere, but now I couldn't tell if he cared either way.

Jacob, through all of this, was lost in thought, still staring at the cube-like desktop sequencer. Jacob resembles Valdimar to some extent—portly and bearded—though older, and probably sharing little common ancestry (not too many Jews in Iceland). "Jónsson," said Jacob, coming out of his reverie, "I've heard of him. The schizophrenic." Jacob glanced at me. He knows about my sister. I looked away.

"He would not identify himself that way," said Valdimar, stroking his beard. "At least not any longer. But yes. Svere Jónsson was diagnosed with schizoaffective disorder as an adolescent. The condition responded to pharmaceutical treatment for many years, but became treatment resistant over the course of a decade. He was an early volunteer for customized gene-modification therapy." All this in perfect, effortless English, which every Icelander appears to possess.

"He was in a condition to volunteer, knowingly, of his own free will?" asked Jacob.

"Free will," repeated Valdimar, neutrally, which I now understood to be his way of laughing in your face. But laughing at what? Perhaps, as a determinist, at the concept itself. This *would* be insulting to Jacob, if he understood how some scientists regard the idea of free will as an illusory crutch, but Jacob just stared at Validmar through his thick glasses, unwitting. Valdimar cracked the tiniest Mona Lisa smile. "Tomorrow, you can ask him yourself."

Thursday, June 10th, 2021

This morning, Jacob, Randall, and I met Ásdís Lúthersdóttir in a park near our hotel (I'd asked Felipe to spend the day at the lab, to learn what he could about the retroviral engineering process). Ásdís grinned and waved to us as we approached, from a bench overlooking a duck pond. She appeared to be in her early fifties, tall, blonde, with a smooth unlined face. The sun at this latitude must be gentle on Caucasian skin.

"We'll take a car from here?" asked Randall, after we'd all introduced ourselves. He stroked his bald head, squinting in the bright light.

"Svere's apartment is very close—we can walk," said Ásdís, and then, seeing Randall's scowl, "Reykjavík is not so large, Mr. Lewis! Not like Houston." She had looked into our backgrounds, and was letting us know.

Along the way Ásdís cheerfully answered our questions, confirming that there was not even a single case of suspected transmission of the gene-altering engineered viruses.

"I'm afraid you don't understand, Mr. Lewis," she said in a way that made me smile, "the virus can *only* replicate within the host it is engineered to infect. And even within the host it dies off as soon as it runs out of cells containing the unaltered target sequence."

"You mean each retrovirus is dependent on the exon sequence it is programmed to modify, in order to replicate?" I asked.

"Not only that. Also a mitochondrial DNA match unique to the individual. A multiple key system, completely secure."

"But the germ line is also modified, right?" said Jacob. "So theoretically, genetic alterations could be passed to the next generation?"

"Not only theoretically, Mr. Weisman, but in actuality. We have two confirmed cases of hereditary transmission of a Hratthníf mod. But that's not a contagion. It has nothing to do with the retrovirus. That's simply procreation."

The day was cool but sunny, and I was enjoying our stroll. We found ourselves in a modest, tidy residential neighborhood, small houses constructed of concrete and colorfully painted sheets of corrugated steel. Lumber, I gather, is in short supply on this island. Probably used up to make all those Viking ships. Ásdís led us to a turquoise metal house, rapped on the door. A tall, burly young man opened it immediately, ushered us in. Svere Jónsson introduced himself, seated us in his living room on a motley assortment of wooden chairs (several of them crudely handmade) and offered us coffee. "It's already made," he said, in a booming voice. "I've been looking forward to your visit."

Ásdís brought us up to speed while Svere clattered away in the kitchen. "Ten years ago psychiatrists began to understand schizophrenia as a disease of overactive neuron pruning, a pathological overdrive of an otherwise normal aspect of brain maturation."

I nodded, familiar with the research because of Wendy. "That's why it often manifests in adolescence or early adulthood, when the brain is thinning out synaptic connections anyway."

"Exactly. The immune system flags certain synapses for destruction with a protein called *complement component 4*, or *C4* for short. Svere was our first volunteer for Hratthníf therapy. We designed his retrovirus to knock out the short form of several C4 genes. This downmodulated expression of the C4 protein, eventually reducing synaptic pruning."

"But wasn't the damage already done?" asked Jacob. "How can altering the genotype do any good if a person has been suffering severe mental illness for years? The brain of a person with long-term schizophrenia *looks* different. You can see it on an MRI."

"All injured brains are constantly trying to repair themselves," said Ásdís. "Schizophrenic brains are no exception."

"It took a few years," said Svere, entering with a tray of steaming coffee cups. Since there was no table, he patiently stooped in front of each of us while we took our white cup and saucer, and cream and sugar if we wanted it. I took mine black. "At first I felt no different, and even when I started to think more clearly, I kept taking my pills. But I don't need them anymore! You might not believe me"—he furrowed his brow, pondering this—"and I guess I can't really prove it. But would you like to see pictures? Then you might understand."

Svere disappeared again, this time into his bedroom, once again making a great deal of noise.

"So if Svere has children, they won't be schizophrenic?" asked Randall, looking up from his phone. He'd been texting somebody. But who? It would be 6 a.m. in D.C. or Atlanta.

"A much reduced chance," said Ásdís. "There is hereditary variability, as well as environmental variables, epigenetic factors. Mental illness is complex, especially when the immune system is involved. One's genotype does not set in stone a particular destiny."

Randall squinted. "And what percentage of schizophrenics in Iceland have received the—what did you call it—the mod?"

"Fourteen have declined."

"Fourteen percent?

"Fourteen individuals. Over ninety-eight percent elected to undergo the therapy."

"And how much does it set them back?" asked Randall, leaning back so far in his handmade chair that it creaked ominously.

"I'm sorry?"

"How much does it *cost*?"

"Oh." Ásdís smiled. "It's completely covered by social insurance. In Iceland, healthcare is free."

Randall glanced at his phone. I'm sure he knew about universal insurance in Iceland. Was he killing time for some reason? Stalling?

"And what is the approximate success rate of the treatment?" I asked. "I realize there may not be clear metrics…"

Svere burst in, carrying a tattered beige photo album. "Eighty percent—myself included—report *complete remission* of symptoms. The other twenty percent *greatly reduced*. It's a cure, simply. More coffee?"

"No thank you."

"Then please, have a look." He offered me the album. "Polaroids of my progress. My caseworker took a picture of my apartment each year, on January 1st."

I took the album, bracing myself, thinking of the squalor I had seen in Wendy's apartment. *Decompensation*, her psychiatrist called it. Completely losing your shit. Not showering for weeks. Not eating. Worse.

"They're in reverse order," said Svere cheerfully. The first page is from this year."

"Svere… how did you learn about the treatment?" asked Jacob.

"*She* told me about it," said Svere, pointing at Ásdís. It was an odd gesture, to point at someone from so close, but didn't seem rude coming from Jónsson, who clearly meant no offense. His social awkwardness again reminded me of my sister. Not necessarily a symptom of the disease, but a side effect of social isolation.

Ásdís nodded slightly. She was sitting up straight, attentive, holding her coffee cup with both hands.

"And you understood the implications, that your personality might change, that there were health risks?" Jacob leaned forward with his line of questioning, staring at Svere with focused intensity.

"Ha! My personality? I *had* no personality. I was terrified of people. I thought everyone was mocking me, or they wanted to hurt me. The treatment gave me my personality *back*."

"Were you in a clear state of mind, to make such a major decision?"

Svere took a seat in the last remaining chair, looked at the floor. "It's hard to explain such a mind state to someone who has never experienced it. Are you asking if I was crazy? Of course I was crazy. I was convinced your government was planting thoughts in my head."

"*My* government?" Jacob frowned.

Svere grinned. "Well, you did *try* to do things like that, didn't you? MK-Ultra and all that? You can't really blame me.

"But even though I was delusional, I wasn't irrational. I realized Ásdís was trying to help me. I trusted her."

Jacob pressed. "Sorry, but it doesn't sound like you were thinking rationally."

Svere defended himself energetically, launching into a long discourse about the nature of logic itself, how delusional thinking can result from *bad information in* (hearing voices and seeing things), not some fault in rational mentation.

I tuned out a little, and with some trepidation opened the photo album in my lap. The first photograph, alone on the page, was a shot of Svere's neat, spare apartment, similar to present day. Handmade wooden chairs, hung paintings of sailboats (painted by Svere himself, I suspected, not unskillfully). The following page, similar, but with fewer paintings and chairs, and some dirty plates on the floor. On the third page the apartment had acquired a ratty brown couch, a battered coffee table topped by an overflowing ashtray. Page four: the floor completely obscured by clothes, cardboard, wood scraps, garbage. I'd seen enough. Images of my sister's defiled bathroom sprang to mind.

"And I understood that the treatment might help me," Svere was saying. "In that way, I was lucid."

Jacob nodded, appearing satisfied by Svere's answer, but I knew him better than to think the matter was closed.

I handed the photo album back to Svere. He took it, smiling ruefully. "Life is good now. Very, very good. I am so grateful to Ásdís."

"State-sanctioned genetic engineering," said Randall. "Nobody in your government has a problem with this?"

I resisted the urge to hurl my remaining coffee at the Texan. He had no idea, the pain of schizophrenia at its worst. The confusion, the word salad, the terrifying hallucinations, the crippling paranoia, the hatred and distrust of family members who love you. The complete lack of motivation, because how can you think about the future when getting through the day is a grueling mountain climb? The very real possibility that you might murder an innocent person because you think they're out to get you. Is it the worst disease? It's crueler than cancer, crueler than dementia. Those end within a few years, one way or another. A severe mental illness might impose fifty years of suffering on an entire family.

"If Iceland can cure schizophrenia within its population, they should." My voice sounded surprisingly calm.

"Yes," said Jacob, stroking his beard in a way that suggested he was about to correct me somehow, "but in a way, it's a form of eugenics. Weeding out undesirable elements from the gene pool."

Ásdís lowered her coffee cup onto its saucer with a sharp clink. "On that point you are mistaken, Mr. Weisman," she said crisply. Was this Icelandic fury? "Eugenics is the practice of sterilizing *individuals* deemed unfit, often for reasons of cultural prejudice completely unrelated to genetic health. The Hratthníf therapy has merely modified a few genes. Svere, the individual, has a *greater* chance of procreation because of it."

Svere had produced a phone and showed Jacob a picture. "It's true! This is my girlfriend Ragna. Trust me, I had a *long* dry stretch before her." I leaned over to get a look, and saw a picture of Svere with his arm around a squat, big-nosed, smiling woman in her late thirties, possibly the least attractive Icelander I'd ever seen. Which is to say, still fairly good-looking.

"What other conditions are you treating?" asked Randall. "I've heard about some. Cystic fibrosis, muscular dystrophy, Huntington's…"

"The complete list is on our website," said Ásdís, no longer tolerating Randall playing dumb.

"And non-disease treatments? Enhancements? Those aren't listed."

"Those aren't yet covered by social insurance, but yes, some non-disease alteration mods are available."

Randall widened his eyes like a cat about to pounce. "And what percentage of the Icelandic population—a rough ballpark—has received these *mods?* Patients—or customers—where no disease was involved."

Ásdís took a slow sip of coffee before answering. "A very small percentage. Generally we Icelanders are happy with our lot in life. We live in an equitable society, with a strong social safety net, and common cultural values shared even by our recent immigrants. Most, if they are experiencing good health, have little desire to modify the genetic hand they were dealt."

"But some have, and they pay privately, and your company is happy to oblige," stated Randall.

"Yes."

"What kind of alterations?" asked Jacob.

"To protect the privacy of our patients, we are not disclosing that information, and we have asked those who have received the treatments to practice discretion. It's one thing to cure a disease, another to design yourself. There's still a strong social bias against the latter. Not so much here in Iceland—we're open-minded when it comes to such things—but our patients could experience discrimination…"

"In backwards religious cultures, like the United States, and Saudi Arabia," interrupted Svere, grinning. "Ásdís is too polite to say what she really means."

"*Design yourself*," repeated Jacob. "Is that what you're calling it?"

"It's completely reckless and arrogant," said Randall, raising his voice, "to introduce new genes into the human gene pool, without at least informing other governments. An international research committee would have been appropriate, something handled via the U.N., with bioethicists like Jacob here. At a *minimum*."

"We are not introducing *new* genes, Mr. Lewis. We are not adding tails to people or making them glow in the dark. All of our mods, to date, are already naturally represented in the global population. Some of them quite rare, but none completely novel.

"And I do not represent the Icelandic government. My work is completely legal within Iceland. That is my only obligation. You may take up your question with the Minister of Foreign Affairs. You're meeting him tomorrow, no?"

"What about your moral obligations, as a scientist? You're *changing* people, in ways that are unpredictable," said Jacob.

"*Life* changes people, Mr. Weisman. Illness, aging, parasites, trauma. It changes them irrevocably, often for the worse. I am perfectly comfortable with the services we are providing. We are helping people, improving their lives. That's why I brought you here, to introduce you to Svere, so you could see for yourself."

"Curing disease is one thing—allowing people to fiddle with their genes for a price is another."

I looked down, feeling embarrassed for Jacob. His questions were earnest but misguided. The Hratthníf therapy was already in use, already showing clear benefits. The ship had sailed.

Ásdís responded patiently. "The modifications are reversible, Mr. Weisman, via the same technique. But so far nobody has elected to reverse any changes."

Reversible. Change your genes (and potentially your body, and brain, and personality, and state of consciousness) as easily as changing clothes. Genetics as fashion.

Randall stood up abruptly. "I can see this is going nowhere quickly." He extended his hand to Svere. "A pleasure to meet you, Mr. Jónsson. Thank you for the coffee." I got the sense that Randall was feigning impatience, that he was playing all of us.

We said our goodbyes, emerged into the bright sunlight. "I'm going to walk," I told the others, checking my map app. "It's only twenty minutes back to our hotel."

"I'll join you," said Jacob.

Ásdís peered over Randall's shoulder at the spinning Uber logo on his phone. "That's not going to work," she said. "The taxi drivers in Iceland are well-unionized. But I can call you one, if you like. They take credit cards."

ɸ

After a quick stop at the hotel I returned to Hratthníf, unannounced. I was recognized and admitted without any security fuss; apparently I had been cleared for unfettered access. Either that, or nobody cared. Odd, considering the potential goldmine the Hratthníf technology represented.

I found Felipe working, unsupervised, at a workstation in the southeast corner of the main floor. Distracted at first by his thick brown hair and the smooth curve of his neck, I only caught a glimpse of his screen as I approached. He appeared to be browsing a raw directory structure.

"Learn anything interesting?"

Felipe quickly closed the file-browsing window before turning to face me. "Hey Jane. Katrín was just showing me their assembler software. She's getting coffee."

"Mind if I sit in?"

He paused, as if confused by my question, and I realized that he was focusing so hard on maintaining direct eye contact that he hadn't heard me.

"I'd like to get a look at the assembler interface myself."

"Oh, of course! Our liaison should be back in a minute. Sorry, I didn't know you were coming by after your meeting. Is Randall here too?"

"No, just me."

Katrín returned shortly with two coffees, and politely offered me her own. I declined, still feeling the effects of Svere's strong brew. Katrín demoed the retrovirus assembler software, which was leagues ahead of anything I'd seen before. But it was hard to concentrate, wondering about Felipe's suspicious behavior.

Friday, June 11th, 2021

The Icelandic Parliament is so close to our hotel that even Randall walked there without complaint. The building is impressive, over 150 years old and hewn of Icelandic dolerite. But, like many things here, also modest and conservative.

Jóhann Gunnarsson, Minister of Foreign Affairs, received us in his office and spent no less than ten minutes (I checked my watch) showing off his wooden boat models to Jacob, whose father had also constructed model boats. Randall sat there fidgeting while we both learned more than we wanted to know about the proper soaking of wood strips prior to curvature. Finally the aide brought us coffee. Randall jumped at the chance to change the subject.

"Mr. Gunnar, I'll get right to the point."

"Gunnarsson. Gunnar is my father." The minister adjusted a boat mast, returned to the seat behind his desk.

Randall cleared his throat. "Sorry. The matter at hand."

"What are the findings of your delegation, so far, Ms. Tokugawa?" asked Gunnarsson, ignoring Randall. He was tall, in his sixties, slightly stooped, once-blond hair graying and thinning.

"We're early in our investigation," I said, "but from what I've learned in regards to how the engineered viruses replicate, the chances of host-to-host transmission are virtually nil."

"Unless it mutates," mumbled Jacob. "That's what viruses *do*."

Gunnarsson smiled. "We understand your concerns, Mr. Weisman. That's why we are fully cooperating with your investigation. Any door that you find shut, you may recruit my help to open."

Gunnarsson's talk of doors opening and shutting triggered a flash of Felipe opening my hotel room door the night before (though not for the reason I'd hoped). Involuntarily I glanced at Randall, who was rubbing his head, nostrils flared.

"Gunnarsson—a blunt question, if I may," said Randall. "Have you licensed this technology to anyone? Other nation states?"

"The Hratthníf gene therapy technology is privately owned, not the government's to license. But no, we understand the technology is sensitive. Such a thing would not be permitted. It could give a single nation too great an advantage."

"But Iceland already *has* that advantage," I pointed out.

"What city are you from, Ms. Tokugawa?"

"Detroit, originally."

"And how many people live there?"

"Now? We're down to about half a million I guess."

"Ah. About the same as Iceland. Some refer to our entire population as a *rounding error*, and there is some truth to that characterization. Other nations are hardly trembling in their boots."

"But you give the treatment to tourists. From any country?" asked Randall.

"We accommodate as many medical tourists as possible. It is our duty to end suffering where we can."

"And what's your policy for tourists who want upgrades? Mods that aren't medically required?"

"We have allowed a certain number of paid visas for such requests. The funds go directly into our general research fund."

"And when they return to their countries of origin, it's with the virus, right? So theoretically it could be extracted and reverse engineered."

"That's not possible," I interrupted, addressing Randall. He didn't seem to understand that each retrovirus was unique.

Randall shrugged. "Jane is the scientist—I'll take her word for it and move on to my next point. Iceland controls this technology exclusively. Many people in the United States with severe illnesses could benefit. Far more than your medical visa program could ever accommodate. Would you consider making an exception to your policy—allow us to make Hratthníf a licensing offer?"

"Let *me* be blunt, Mr. Lewis. Are you brokering a deal for a U.S. corporation?"

Randall shook his head brusquely, but didn't seem offended. "The money would come out of the federal budget. We'd offer the service via Medicare, license it throughout our private provider networks. The U.S. government would save billions in healthcare costs, preventing or curing illnesses and chronic long-term conditions."

Only yesterday Randall was railing at Ásdís Lúthersdóttir about the dangers of introducing new material into the human gene pool. But Felipe's late-night confession had prepared me for this about-face. I understood what was going on, and I felt a cold rage as I considered how I was being used.

Gunnarsson pursed his lips. "I would consider it, Mr. Lewis. You're right. Many more people could be helped. But I have a question. Would you want an exclusive license, or non-exclusive?" He smiled thinly.

Lewis shrugged. "Probably exclusive, for a limited time, with the exception of your own country's use, of course."

⚜

I'd opened the door at 4 a.m. to Felipe, pale and drawn. He asked if he could come in. I offered him a drink courtesy of the U.S. taxpayer. We chose Brennivín from the minibar, and found the licorice flavor surprisingly mild for a drink named after *Yersinia pestis*.

"You know, don't you?" he blurted. "I'm sorry. I should have turned him down. I feel terrible. I'm a good person, Jane. And so are the people at Hratthníf. I saw a video of the boy with Duchenne…"

"Whoa—slow down. Start from the beginning."

Randall Lewis had recruited him, early on, to conduct corporate espionage against Hratthníf. Felipe had been tasked with stealing the plans for the desktop sequencer, or even better, obtaining a physical model. Randall had paid him with a block of crisp hundred-dollar bills, with the same amount to come should Felipe complete his mission. Intimidated by Randall, but also thrilled at the prospect of serving his nation as a spy, Felipe had yet to even count the money.

"Was Randall texting you yesterday?"

"Yes—to tell me he was keeping Ásdís Lúthersdóttir busy off-site."

"But you've decided not to help him? That's why you're here, talking to me?"

"No! I've already done it. I thought you knew. When Katrín was getting coffee I did some network snooping, found a bunch of schematic and engineering files, even some source code. I copied it all onto a thumb drive."

"That sounds too easy. Decoy files, probably. You walked right into a honeypot."

Felipe shrugged. "Maybe. But they do seem very trusting. And the company doesn't seem super organized. Maybe they just haven't gotten around to network security."

I nodded. There was a chance he was right.

"I feel terrible stealing from them. Their company really does have an altruistic mission. Katrín showed me before-and-after videos of a French boy, Jacques, with Duchenne muscular dystrophy. He used a wheelchair, was having breathing troubles. They fixed his DMD gene. *Fully repaired it.* Jane, he was *running around* two years later. It made me cry."

I let Felipe unburden his guilt, listened patiently, told him to sit tight, not tell Randall anything. I gave him a hug and (reluctantly) sent him back to his room.

$

In Gunnarsson's office, I turned to Randall, furious. He wasn't even bothering to maintain the facade that we were here for an *investigation*. "You no longer have concerns about *state-sanctioned genetic engineering?*" I said archly. Gunnarsson raised an eyebrow, leaned back in his chair.

"Not after talking to Lúthersdóttir, no," said Randall, keeping his tone even. Jacob frowned at me.

Jacob cleared his throat. "Mr. Gunnarsson, if it's not too personal, would you mind telling us if you've received any of the Hratthníf mods? And if so, which ones?"

"Hratthníf advises us not to, but it's our choice. I don't mind telling you at all. I've received four, in fact. The first was to correct a gene involved in mast cell production. I've struggled with asthma since I was a boy. It didn't work, at first. But I took another therapy, a stem cell injection, also from Hratthníf. Something to reset my immune system. It worked—I don't use an inhaler anymore. A huge blessing.

"The second corrected a mutation in a cursed gene called Q141K. One that resulted in years of excruciating pain in my left toe. To the point where I could barely walk, my friends. You've heard of uric acid, I'm sure? Well, I had too much of it. The gout. And it wasn't due to rich food either—I ate nothing but salads for a year trying to get better, abstained from all alcohol. But now, I eat and drink what I want." He grinned, gesturing to a nearby shelf of whiskey. Fine Islay Scotch, most of it, and a 12-year Yamazaki.

"The third I was nervous about, but I was hardly the first to try it. You've heard of the APOE gene? It's involved in Alzheimer's, but also memory in general, even for young people. I now carry the epsilon-4 allele, and my memory is a little sharper. Not a huge effect, but significant. If they had a *genius* mod, I'd go for it, but that's not on the menu yet."

I thought of Iceland's recent achievements in the arts and sciences. Maybe there wasn't a genius mod. Or maybe they just hadn't offered it to Gunnarsson.

"The last, well, it's a little embarrassing. I can't remember the name of it, but it's a gene that regulates nitric oxide synthase."

Jacob chuckled.

"What's so funny?" asked Randall.

"Yes—he understands!" said Gunnarsson. "The mod is prescribed for vascular health and reducing blood pressure, ostensibly. But there are other benefits my wife could tell you about."

"It sounds as if a single research lab in Iceland has made big pharma obsolete," I pointed out.

"If we were licensing the technology globally, that might be the case. It's a big reason we haven't. We're not trying to make enemies or change things too quickly."

"But the world wants what you have. And it *will* get it, eventually," said Randall.

Gunnarsson stiffened, but maintained his composure. "We won't stand in the way of progress, Mr. Lewis. We're willing to make a deal. With your help on one matter, I think I could make the case to our parliament to allow your government to negotiate directly with Hratthnif."

"What do you want?"

"Our ethicists are drafting an amendment to the Human Rights Charter."

"The U.N.?" asked Jacob.

"Exactly. An amendment adding the right of genetic self-determination."

Randall frowned. "You're talking mass access to the technology. We're not there yet, nowhere near."

"Things can move quickly, Mr. Lewis, as you just implied. The world wants what we have. We might as well get the ethical infrastructure in place."

"To consider the ethics makes sense," said Jacob, "but I have some serious concerns."

I caught Gunnarsson checking his watch as Jacob elucidated those concerns in detail, though when the meeting finally concluded the two men lingered for a minute to exchange thoughts on model boat rigging. Outside, Randall said a quick goodbye and hopped in an already-waiting taxi. I waited until Jacob emerged from the building and the two of us took a stroll alongside a small lake directly in front of the parliament building. We walked in silence for some time, composing our thoughts and observing the local avian life. Icelandic birds have long, curved tail feathers. Maybe to better navigate the harsh ocean winds.

"What was your impression of Gunnarsson?" I asked.

"Sincere. I like him. But I don't think he has any idea what the larger implications are, of this technology going mainstream."

"Which are?"

"Mass at-will self-editing of the genome? That doesn't concern you?"

"What concerns you about it?" I was feeling defensive, because of the possibility that the Hratthníf therapy might help Wendy, but I tried to keep my feelings in check.

"What if everyone just chooses genes that make them happy all the time? Without human striving and ambition, progress could grind to a halt."

"I'm pretty sure psychologists have found the opposite to be true—positive feelings are associated with productivity and creativity. And if Iceland's recent achievements are any measure, we don't have to worry about some kind of happiness-induced collapse of civilization."

Jacob sighed, exasperated. "Okay, bad example. What really worries me is what our military is going to do with this tech once they get ahold of it."

"You mean genetic super-soldiers?"

"So what if they're stronger or faster, but what if they start knocking out genes involved in empathy? Turn regular soldiers into psychopaths… more effective killers."

"Well, that's a nightmarish idea. But honestly I don't think there's any shortage of psychopaths applying for military service already. Not all of them, obviously, but *enough*, if you're thinking about recruiting for dirty work."

A gaggle of mostly blond bicycle-riding children passed us, chattering excitedly in Icelandic.

"You know we're being used, right?" I said. "There's no valid cause for an investigation. There's no contagion here, no *disease*."

Jacob frowned. "Can we be sure of that? Viruses can mutate."

I explained Hratthníf's double-key system (exon identification plus host-specific mitochondrial DNA matching) in more detail.

"So the point of this entire expedition is to broker a deal? So the U.S. government can get access to Hratthníf?"

"Yes." I considered telling Jacob about the data theft, but decided against it for the moment. I wasn't sure how he would react, and I hadn't yet decided what *I* was going to do about it.

"And should we? Do you believe Lewis, with all his talk about preventative medicine and making the therapy widely available?"

"I don't know. I don't fully trust him. Your super-soldier conspiracy theory might not be so far off base."

Jacob stopped in his tracks. "So where are we on this? What's the right thing to do here?"

I gestured to a nearby bench. We sat. I put on sunglasses to filter the bright morning light. Jacob squinted, suppressed a sneeze.

"It's coming, one way or another," I said. "The ability to edit your own genome, at will. The issue is access—which nations and social classes get first dibs. Right now, the citizens of Iceland and medical tourists are the only ones who can receive the therapy."

"And they seem to be using it responsibly, so far," said Jacob.

"Agreed. And from what Gunnarsson said, they'd like to see wide access be the default. A new human right."

"That's idealistic to the point of naiveté."

"Maybe. But Iceland keeps surprising the world with its pragmatic idealism."

Jacob growled, clenched his fists. "Doesn't it *bother* you, an island nation of blond Nordic people recklessly hurtling down the path of complete genetic self-determination? *Aryans.* Nations pursuing eugenic agendas hasn't ended well in the past. My grandfather escaped on the Kindertransport—the rest of his family was killed. It wasn't that long ago."

"It's not eugenics. Lúthersdóttir isn't some crazed Icelandic Mengele. And they're not all blond." At the airport I'd heard an Asian woman speak fluent Icelandic; it had surprised me. A racist reaction, no different than white Americans asking me *Where are you from?*

"I know what Ásdís said, but it's still messing with your genes. It's saying that parts of you *aren't good enough.*"

I shook my head. "There's a real opportunity here to relieve suffering."

"What would you change?"

"What?"

"If you could change any part of your genetic makeup, what would you change?"

The question caught me off guard. I had thought only of how the therapy might help Wendy. Or more specifically, how it might help *me*, by helping Wendy. Giving me my sister back, the one I remembered from childhood, happy and outgoing and pretty and smarter than any of us.

"Nothing, I guess."

"You're fine the way you are."

"I'm comfortable with my flaws."

"What if the state disagreed? Mandated genetic therapy to save on long-term health expenses."

"I'd want the right to choose."

"Of course you would."

Jacob grunted, satisfied that his point had been made, though I wasn't sure what point he was trying to make. Maybe that we couldn't anticipate the consequences of letting this particular cat out of the bag.

Monday, June 14th, 2021

We all agreed to take the weekend off. Randall went completely dark—no email, texts, or calls. I caught only glimpses of him passing in the hotel lobby. Jacob, Felipe, and I enjoyed a few of Iceland's many tourist attractions, including the Viking settlement unearthed during the construction of our hotel. Yesterday Jacob went solo on a tour to soak in the famous Blue Lagoon. I had no desire to get on another crowded, overheated shuttle bus, so Felipe and I stayed in town to check out Laugardalslaug, a local swimming pool/waterpark. The facility was impressive, featuring a number of large geothermally-heated pools and a twisty waterslide filled with psychedelic lights. As I suspected, Felipe looks great in a bathing suit. We flirted a little, avoiding work talk (and his confession) altogether. By dinnertime Jacob wasn't yet back from the Blue Lagoon, so Felipe and I went out, had some food and a few drinks. I tried to make it obvious that I was up for more than flirting, but I don't think I got through. Either that or he's just not interested.

This morning I received a text from Randall, instructing me to meet him immediately at a GPS map point near the docks, a ten-minute walk from our hotel. I considered delaying or ignoring the missive—I didn't like him ordering me around—but my curiosity won out. *On my way*, I texted back.

My map app led me to a historic exhibit near the water, an array of signs mounted atop concrete blocks, each with a map of Iceland, indicating the exact location, date, and reason for every shipwreck within a particular decade. I felt I was beginning to get a sense of the national character— it seemed *Icelandic* to process tragedy via meticulous record keeping and public infographics.

Randall was already there, standing next to a shipwreck sign and typing into his phone. Seeing me, he reached into his pocket and retrieved a folded piece of paper. "Here." He thrust it at me. "Key points to cover in your report."

I unfolded the note, handwritten on our hotel stationary in Randall's neat, blocky print. Twelve bullet-points. The gist of it: Hratthníf's line of research was reckless and irresponsible, their protocols sloppy and hazardous, the result being a significant risk to public health, both in Iceland and globally.

I refolded the paper. "This is ridiculous. The engineered viruses aren't transmissible. If what Lúthersdóttir has told us about the double key system is true—and I'm going to verify that it *is*—then there really is nothing to worry about. At least not from the point of view of the CDC."

"Put it in your own words. Whatever language you need to use. Just make sure you sell it. It's *not* safe. You don't even have to get into the contagion aspect of it."

"There *is* no contagion." I couldn't help myself from arguing, even though at this point I realized Randall didn't believe any of his own bullet points. He wanted a negative report on file from the CDC, something to provide leverage for his negotiations. Hurt Hratthníf's reputation, drive down the company's value so he could snap up the gene therapy technology at a discount. I resisted the urge to rip the paper in half, instead tucked it in my jeans pocket. "I won't write a false report."

He closed the distance between us, grabbed my upper arm. "You *will* write the report I need you to write. The report *your country* needs you to write. Do you have any idea what's at stake here? This is a fucking global tipping point. In the next few years, everything changes. Your actions matter, Ms. Tokugawa. They matter a great deal."

"Let go of me."

He released me, took a single step back. "Your sister will be among the first to receive the therapy. I'll make sure of it."

That caught me. I stopped breathing for a moment. "And if I refuse?"

"You won't refuse. You'll make the right decision, because I'll persuade you to make it. That's what I do." He rapped his knuckles on the 1890s shipwreck sign for emphasis, strode off without looking back.

I stood there trembling, my body reacting to the threat. To what lengths was he willing to go? Would he make sure Wendy would be *denied* the Hratthníf therapy if I refused to cooperate? Would he threaten violence, against me or Wendy? Had he just done so, obliquely?

I didn't really think Randall needed a negative report from the CDC. The State Department would obtain the Hratthníf technology one way or another, via trade, espionage, whatever means were necessary.

Randall needed to know he could control me. Maybe he knew that I was on to him.

My bloodstream was coursing with adrenaline, but I wasn't scared. *Resolve* is what I felt. I would not be a pawn in his game.

⚵

Felipe opened his hotel door, sleepy-eyed, buttoning his shirt. "Do we have something today? I don't have anything on my calendar until…"

"May I come in?"

I shut the door behind me. "Give me everything you have. All of it. Did you make copies? Did you say anything to Randall?"

He hadn't made copies, or talked to Randall. He handed me the thumb drive with palpable relief.

"Tell Randall you tried but failed. Security was too tight."

"I'll give him the money back if he asks. I shouldn't have agreed to it. I feel awful."

"Keep the money. You earned it." I leaned in, kissed him on the lips before he could react.

"Huh?"

"More tonight, if you want."

Back in my room, I copied the files to my laptop, encrypted them, tucked the thumb drive into my jeans pocket next to Randall's note. I'd find a way to destroy the drive later. The note I would keep as evidence.

I browsed Felipe's stolen cache. Much of it seemed to be in proprietary formats, but after a few minutes researching file extensions I realized the bulk of it was open-source database and CAD files, and unencrypted text. Felipe had grabbed whatever he could, nearly filling the two terabyte drive. It was a massive haul. But was it real?

I dug deeper, reading research papers and case studies, my laptop translating as needed. The holy grail would be the machine schematics for the desktop sequencer. Or some kind of master list of all the mods offered. After an hour I found the former, in a directory simply entitled *Machine*. Almost too straightforward for a honeypot.

I didn't yet know the extent of what I had, but *I* had it, not Randall. As a precaution I created an encrypted archive and uploaded it to an anonymous file-sharing site, privately linked.

At that point I became aware of two paths, two possible futures. But I needed to talk to Ásdís Lúthersdóttir one more time before making my decision.

Tuesday, June 15th, 2021

Felipe knocked softly around one in the morning, kissed me as soon as I opened the door. The sex lived up to my considerable expectations and provided a welcome distraction. It wasn't only physical—afterwards we talked for hours about our lives and families and hopes and fears. He's asleep in my bed now. I won't sleep until I've made my decision, won't even try.

$ \maltese $

Felipe is at Hratthníf, meeting with Valdimar to review the mitochondrial DNA-matching algorithm that confines each individually constructed retrovirus to a single host. Jacob is meeting with the Minister of Health to confirm Hratthníf's claims that there are no reported cases of host transmission (or any other dark secrets—nasty side effects or unexplained illnesses).

I have an appointment with Lúthersdóttir at 4 p.m. Texted her to meet me at the waterpark. Seems safe there, no chance we'll be overheard by anyone who would care. If she was suspicious of my motivations she didn't let on, wrote back that an afternoon swim sounded fun.

$

Walked around Reykjavík, alone, people watching. Icelanders may be taller and fitter and blonder, on average, than Americans, but the full spectrum of human variety is on display here. If there is more spring in their step, that might be an effect of summer, the preternatural light. I felt it myself; despite my sleep-deprived state I was alert and energized.

We still have no idea how many Icelanders have received Hratthníf mods of one sort or another. Despite what Gunnarsson said about Icelanders generally being happy with their lot in life, the percentage might be quite high. Who wouldn't fix a genetic flaw or two, if they could? I'd reconsidered Jacob's question about what *I* would change. If I could, I might flip a switch to permanently end my seasonal allergies. Gunnarsson's memory boost sounded useful as well.

Maybe Iceland's surge in productivity and creativity can be attributed to fewer niggling health complaints, plus a few percentage points of enhanced mental acuity. No *genius mod*—just a nation enjoying the cumulative benefits of minor genetic optimization.

Pedestrian was the word that came to mind, to describe what I had learned of how the elective mods might be used. Gunnarsson's *old man* fixes: gout, memory, better performance in the sack. What was *reckless* about that? Nothing dangerous there, unless you were a pharmaceutical company about to watch your profits disappear into the void.

But the medical mods—that was the game changer. An ocean of silent suffering relieved, for individuals (and their families and caregivers) suffering from severe mental illness, muscular dystrophy, other miseries inflicted by broken genes. All now fixable.

I wouldn't let Randall get in the way of that.

ϕ

Just returned from the waterpark. Feeling relaxed, though I haven't yet pulled the trigger.

Ásdís met me in front of Laugardalslaug. We walked in together, paid the modest fee, received our locker wristbands, made our way to the changing room. We undressed next to one another, chatting. It didn't feel awkward. Even in the showers (required, for pool hygiene) I felt oddly comfortable in the nude in front of strangers. Maybe a residual effect of sleeping with Felipe this morning.

Swimsuits on, we waded into one of the hot tub areas, taking over a semi-private curved seating area. Ásdís made small talk, asked how our delegation was enjoying Iceland, waited for me to broach the topic of why I had asked her there. Though I suspected she knew.

"Has Lewis made you an offer yet?" I asked, after a natural break in our conversation.

"Not only made, but accepted. And the funds already transferred. Your government works quickly, Jane."

I frowned. I hadn't expected this. "What terms did you agree to?"

"Exclusive license of the retroviral genetic modification therapy outside of Iceland, though we're free to continue serving our own population, and some number of medical tourists. Our stem-cell therapies and other research lines are not part of the deal."

"Were you… coerced?"

Ásdís smiled thinly. "Lewis made it clear he wouldn't take no for an answer, but the price he offered was high enough. You're looking at a very rich woman. Me, and all my employees, and all our investors. I'm an entrepreneur as well as a scientist. There was no need to coerce me."

I nodded and looked away as the disappointment sunk in. I had misjudged Lúthersdóttir. She was just a mercenary. But I also felt relief—Randall would no longer need a falsified, alarmist report from the CDC to use as leverage. The deal was already done. Across the heated pool a young man bent his knees so that his head descended beneath the surface.

I decided to speak my mind. "It's possible that you've condemned millions of people to continued suffering. There's no guarantee the U.S. government will make the Hratthníf therapy widely available. We might use it for military purposes. Or reserve its use for the elite political class and their financial backers."

Ásdís grunted. "Worse than that. Lewis intends to kill the technology altogether. He'd shut down our research in Iceland too, if he had the clout. He still intends to, in fact."

"Why do you think that?"

"He's on the payroll of five major U.S. pharmaceutical companies. The payments are buried through stacked LLC chains, but our legal team traced them. We looked into each of you quite extensively when we received your delegation's request for access. I knew it was the beginning of the end game."

"Then why…"

"If you're concerned about your sister, I can arrange a medical visa for her. We work closely with immigration services, try to prioritize the most critical cases."

I was having trouble composing my thoughts. The young man who had submerged his head was still underwater. How long could he hold his breath?

"I don't understand," I said simply. "I asked you here because there's something I've been considering doing—something extreme, but I didn't want to negatively impact your efforts. You're doing good work here in Iceland. Why limit the technology?"

"Your colleague Felipe missed a few things. When you return to your hotel room you'll find a link to a more complete archive with all the assets you'll need. We've also compiled a distribution list. Journalists, medical journals, open-source fabrication sites, the like."

The man was still underwater. "You *want* me to leak the schematics?"

"The schematics, the source code, the basic research, all of it. Unless I've misjudged your intent? The files Felipe stole are incomplete, the designs flawed. We took precautions—we weren't sure who he was working for. Randall Lewis, I presume, his Plan B in case negotiations fell through?"

"Yes, though Felipe had a change of heart."

"To be direct, we want your help distributing the files. We could do it ourselves, but it's safer if it looks like a breach. You've provided us with such an opportunity, according to our network logs."

"You want the technology to be freely available. Released into the wild."

"Millions could be helped. It's the right thing to do."

I frowned, considering this. Once again, I was being used, a pawn in a larger game. But on the right side this time.

"Randall Lewis will be furious. And you'll lose millions in royalties."

"We Icelanders are not defenseless. And the money"—she laughed lightly—"now we have much more than we need."

Finally the man across from us surfaced. Water streamed from his hair down his face, rippled along the sides of neck, down his shoulders. Strangely, he did not even seem out of breath. Perhaps he had quietly hyperventilated before submerging.

"That man held his breath for a very long time."

Ásdís, waving at someone she had just recognized, didn't hear me.

$
In

At the internet cafe I finished the last of my coffee, reviewed the short message I'd written on the anonymous email site. As promised, I'd found a plain envelope tucked under my hotel room door. A single sheet of paper with a handwritten abbreviated URL. I'd typed it in my browser window, confirmed that Ásdís had meant what she'd said.

I hadn't told Jacob or Felipe, though not for lack of trust. I didn't want to put either man in unnecessary danger in case Randall Lewis decided to retaliate. This was my decision, my burden.

I checked the link once more, compared it to the handwritten note. Who had written it? Ásdís herself? Who else was in on the conspiracy? Gunnarsson? The entire Icelandic parliament? I scanned the contents of the Bcc field. It had taken twenty minutes to type in all the addresses. I clicked Send. The deed was done.

I glanced around the cafe. Nobody was paying me any attention. Changing the course of history felt anticlimactic. A wave of fatigue, and all I wanted in life was to shuffle back to my hotel room, crawl in bed.

Thursday, June 17th, 2021

Randall left yesterday on a private jet. He let Jacob know via text. No contact with me. There's nothing in the press yet, but that doesn't mean he hasn't found out.

The shuttle back to Keflavík wasn't crowded, and I spread out my stuff on the aisle seat so that neither Felipe nor Jacob could sit next to me. But both were content to sit by themselves. Felipe has been polite but a little distant, maybe trying to reestablish out professional relationship. Jacob just looked exhausted.

Iceland's landscape seemed different this time, the lichen colors more vivid, the contours of the volcanic rock more defined. I wondered if I would be returning soon with my sister. I'd received an email from Gunnarsson himself, with instructions for applying for a medical visa, and assurances that he would personally expedite the processing. Expenses would be covered or reimbursed.

Would Wendy even *want* to go? Maybe she was happy enough, managing with her meds and caseworker support. Change can be terrifying.

Ahead, on the side of the road, I noticed a broad-shouldered, long-haired man watching our bus approach. Time slowed as we passed him, an illusion produced by my brain's hyperkinetic attempt to process the visual information it was receiving. The man was strangely clad, wearing only a fur vest, loincloth, and boots—maybe made of sealskin. His own skin was a deep blue-green color, not unlike the lichen-encrusted rocks behind him. He looked me directly in the eye, his blue skin stretching over the striated musculature of his exposed chest as he lifted a massive arm and waved. There was not an ounce of fat on his torso. Still waving, he grinned widely, revealing two rows of shark-like teeth.

And then we were past him. Even craning my neck, I could not get another glimpse of the man. "Did you…" I leaned out into the aisle. Felipe was reading. Jacob was asleep.

What had Ásdís said? *Design yourself. We are open-minded about such things.* Perhaps from the heat and the motion, I began to feel sick. I made my way to the front of the bus.

"Could you please turn down the heat?" I asked the driver.

"Of course. No problem," the driver replied, in the friendly, reasonable tone I had become accustomed to hearing from Icelandic people.

Acknowledgments

Some thanks are due here. First of all, to my mother Linda Lancione, who I deeply respect as a writer. She gave me valuable feedback on this story, and also recommended that I submit it to the Omnidawn Fabulist Fiction Contest. Good call Mom.

I'd also like to thank all my readers, especially my wife Kia (who usually gets the first and worst version). Thank you to Rob English, with whom I exchange critiques weekly. And also to Jason Wohlstadter and Jason Kleidosty, for always being up for reading my work and telling me what they think.

Another thank you to Kia, and to my daughter Tesla Rose, and to my entire family, who enthusiastically and consistently cheer on my fiction writing.

Thank you to the people of Iceland, especially the friendly staff at Laugardalslaug.

And finally, thanks to Bradford Morrow and the readers of the Omnidawn Fabulist Fiction Contest—I'm glad they saw the value in this story. And to Rusty, Ken, Gillian, and everyone else at Omnidawn, who are a pleasure to work with.

J.D. Moyer lives in Oakland, California, with his wife, daughter, and mystery-breed dog. He writes science fiction, produces electronic music in two groups (Jondi & Spesh and Momu), runs a record label (Loöq Records), and blogs at jdmoyer.com. His previous stories have appeared in *The Magazine of Fantasy & Science Fiction*, *Strange Horizons*, *The InterGalactic Medicine Show*, and *Cosmic Roots And Eldritch Shores*. His first novel, *The Sky Woman*, will be published in late 2018 (Flame Tree).

The Icelandic Cure
by J.D. Moyer

Cover photo: "The Eye of the Tiger," Christian Gloor.

Cover and interior set in Myriad Pro and Adobe Garamond Pro

Cover and interior design by Gillian Olivia Blythe Hamel

Offset printed in the United States
by Edwards Brothers Malloy, Ann Arbor, Michigan
On 55# Glatfelter B18 Antique
Acid Free Archival Quality Recycled Paper

Publication of this book was made possible in part by gifts from:
The New Place Fund
The Clorox Company Foundation

Omnidawn Publishing
Oakland, California
2018
Rusty Morrison & Ken Keegan, senior editors & co-publishers
Trisha Peck, managing editor & program director
Gillian Olivia Blythe Hamel, senior poetry editor
Cassandra Smith, poetry editor & book designer
Sharon Zetter, poetry editor, book designer & development officer
Liza Flum, poetry editor
Avren Keating, poetry editor & fiction editor
Juliana Paslay, fiction editor
Gail Aronson, fiction editor
Tinia Montford, marketing assistant
Emily Alexander, marketing assistant
Terry A. Taplin, marketing assistant
Matthew Bowie, marketing assistant
SD Sumner, copyeditor

THE
ICELANDIC
CURE

J.D. MOYER
THE ICELANDIC CURE

OMNIDAWN PUBLISHING
OAKLAND, CALIFORNIA
2018

Cover photo: "The Eye of the Tiger," Christian Gloor.

Cover and interior set in Myriad Pro and Adobe Garamond Pro

Cover and interior design by Gillian Olivia Blythe Hamel

Offset printed in the United States
by Edwards Brothers Malloy, Ann Arbor, Michigan
On 55# Glatfelter B18 Antique
Acid Free Archival Quality Recycled Paper

Library of Congress Cataloging-in-Publication Data

Names: Moyer, J. D., 1969- author.
Title: The Icelandic Cure / J. D. Moyer.
Other titles: Icelandic cure
Description: Oakland, California : Omnidawn Publishing, [2018]
Identifiers: LCCN 2017051236 | ISBN 9781632430519 (pbk. : alk. paper)
Subjects: LCSH: Women scientists--Fiction. | Gene therapy--Fiction. |
  Retroviruses--Fiction.
Classification: LCC PS3613.O9244 I23 2018 | DDC 813/.6--dc23
LC record available at https://lccn.loc.gov/2017051236

Published by Omnidawn Publishing, Oakland, California
www.omnidawn.com   (510) 237-5472   (800) 792-4957
10 9 8 7 6 5 4 3 2 1
ISBN: 978-1-63243-51-9